MAR 1 2 2008

W9-ADU-691

Jeremy Kreep

FANG FAIRY

written and illustrated by Andy J. Smith

Librarian Reviewer
Katharine Kan
Graphic novel reviewer and Library Consultant, Panama City, FL
MLS in Library and Information Studies, University of Hawaii at
Manoa, HI

Reading Consultant
Elizabeth Stedem
Educator/Consultant, Colorado Springs, CO
MA in Elementary Education, University of Denver, CO

▟▙ STONE ARCH BOOKS
MINNEAPOLIS   SAN DIEGO

Graphic Sparks are published by Stone Arch Books
151 Good Counsel Drive, P.O. Box 669
Mankato, Minnesota 56002
www.stonearchbooks.com

Copyright © 2008 by Stone Arch Books

All rights reserved. No part of this publication may be reproduced
in whole or in part, or stored in a retrieval system, or transmitted in any
form or by any means, electronic, mechanical, photocopying, recording,
or otherwise, without written permission of the publisher.

Library of Congress Cataloging-in-Publication Data
Smith, Andy J., 1975–
    Fang Fairy / by Andy J. Smith; illustrated by Andy J. Smith.
    p. cm. — (Graphic Sparks. Jeremy Kreep)
    ISBN-13: 978-1-59889-835-4 (library binding)
    ISBN-10: 1-59889-835-3 (library binding)
    ISBN-13: 978-1-59889-891-0 (paperback)
    ISBN-10: 1-59889-891-4 (paperback)
    1. Graphic novels. I. Title.
PN6727.S5456F36 2008
741.5'973—dc22   2007003176

Summary: Jeremy Kreep has a problem. Something snagged a baby tooth from beneath his
brother's pillow and left a puddle of slime! Now Jeremy and his best friend Nessy go off
to find the truth behind the tooth fairy. Is the creature just a silly superstition or a real-life
collector of fangs?

Art Director: Heather Kindseth
Graphic Designer: Brann Garvey

1 2 3 4 5 6 12 11 10 09 08 07

Printed in the United States of America

Jeremy Kreep

FANG FAIRY

written and illustrated
by Andy J. Smith

Genoa City Public Library
P.O. Box 727
126 Freeman St.
Genoa City, WI 53128
262-279-6188

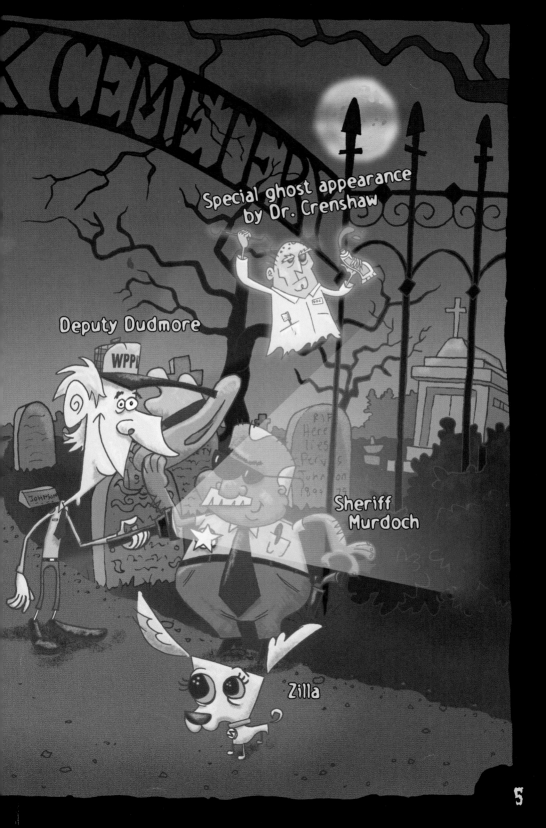

It's another ordinary night in Widow's Peak, Nebraska.

But the nights in Widow's Peak are never completely **ordinary** . . .

WELCOME TO
WIDOW'S PEAK
EST. 1807
POPULATION 665 %

7

Genoa City Public Library

CREEEEK

I'll turn on the lights.

FLICK!

25

27

When I found Zilla, his leg was broken and all his teeth were missing. After I passed away, nobody could protect him.

Yeah, I don't suppose anyone's scared by a tiny Chihuahua with no teeth.

And bad breath!

So I came back from the grave for my last great dental procedure and surgically implanted these new teeth!

That dental glue you used is the green slime!

And it's mint flavored.

29

That's just another ordinary day in Widow's Peak, Nebraska.

Down the road from Heck.

ABOUT THE AUTHOR AND ILLUSTRATOR

From a young age, Andy Smith knew he wanted to be an illustrator (if he couldn't be a space adventurer, superhero, or ghost hunter). After graduating from college in 1998, he began working at a handful of New York City animation studios on shows like *Courage the Cowardly Dog* and *Sheep in the Big City*, while also working in freelance illustration. Andy has since left New York City for Rochester, NY, where he teaches high school art and illustration at the Rochester Institute of Technology.

GLOSSARY

Chihuahua (chi-WAH-wah)—a breed of very small dogs with big eyes and pointed ears

digital camera (DIJ-uh-tul KAM-ur-uh)—a machine that captures photographs electronically instead of using film. A digital camera stores its pictures on a computer chip.

evidence (EV-uh-duhnss)—facts or info that help prove that something is true

mongrel (MONG-gruhl)—a dog that is a mixture of different breeds

stakeout (STAYK-out)—watching an area to catch a criminal in the act

tofu (TOH-foo)—a soft food made from soybeans

willies (WIHL-eez)—a nervous feeling about a situation; also called the **jitters**, the **heebie-jeebies,** and the **creepy crawlies**.

yowza (YOW-zuh)—something you might say when you get the willies!

SOME TOOTH TRUTH

Here are just a few truths about the tooth.

Like Zilla the Chihuahua, the first U.S. president, George Washington, had fake teeth. Many believe they were made from wood. They were actually made from gold, ivory, lead, and even whale bone!

Don't blame Washington for his bad teeth, though. The first modern toothbrush wasn't invented until 1780 in England. Americans didn't start brushing daily for another 150 years!

Before the first toothbrush, people kept their teeth clean by chewing on twigs.

In parts of the world, straight, white teeth are not popular. People in some Asian countries color their teeth black. In some parts of Africa, people file their teeth into sharp points.

Humans get two sets of teeth in their lifetime. The first set of 20 teeth are often called primary teeth, baby teeth, or milk teeth.

Grown-up humans have 32 teeth, but dogs have that number beat. Adult dogs have 42 teeth.

Around the world, children have different ways for getting rid of teeth that fall out. In the United States, kids often leave them under a pillow for the tooth fairy. Other countries have a "tooth mouse" that scurries around collecting baby teeth. Some South American children even have their old teeth made into jewelry.

DISCUSSION QUESTIONS

1.) Jeremy and Nessy were scared when they first met Zilla the Chihuahua. Have you ever judged someone on how they look? Do you think this is wrong? Why?

2.) Dr. Crenshaw's ghost stole children's teeth to help Zilla the Chihuahua. Is stealing ever okay? Explain your answer.

3.) Why do you think the author chose a Chihuahua as the Hound from Heck? Explain your answer. What type of dog would you have chosen?

WRITING PROMPTS

1.) Zilla howls like a wolf and has some pretty wacky teeth. List three things that make your own pet or your friend's pet unique. Write a story about the pet using these three features.

2.) Have you ever tried to solve a mystery like Jeremy and Nessy did? Did you solve it? Describe the mystery and your solution.

3.) This story focuses on just one day in the town of Widow's Peak, Nebraska. Write a story about another day in the strange town. What crazy things happen on that day?

INTERNET SITES

Do you want to know more about subjects related to this book? Or are you interested in learning about other topics? Then check out FactHound, a fun, easy way to find Internet sites.

Our investigative staff has already sniffed out great sites for you!

Here's how to use FactHound:

1. Visit *www.facthound.com*

2. Select your grade level.

3. To learn more about subjects related to this book, type in the book's ISBN number: **1598898353**.

4. Click the **Fetch It** button.

FactHound will fetch the best Internet sites for you!